EVERYTHING GLISTENS AND EVERYTHING SINGS

Charlotte Zolotow

EVERYTHING GLISTENS
AND EVERYTHING SINGS

NEW AND SELECTED POEMS

ILLUSTRATED BY

Margot Tomes

HARCOURT BRACE JOVANOVICH, PUBLISHERS

SAN DIEGO   NEW YORK   LONDON

To Anna Bier
and Lee Bennett Hopkins
with affection and gratitude

HBJ

"Little Bird," "Autumn," "In Bed," and "The Spring Wind" are from *River Winding* by Charlotte Zolotow (T. Y. Crowell), Copyright © 1970 by Charlotte Zolotow. Reprinted by permission of the publisher.

"Crocus," "These Things" (now retitled "Candlelight and Moth Wings"), "Halfway Where I'm Going," "The Top and the Tip," "Look," "Weeds," "School Day," "People," "The Boats," "Summer Snow," "The Fireflies," and "The Apple Tree" are from *All That Sunlight* by Charlotte Zolotow, Copyright © 1967 by Charlotte Zolotow. Reprinted by permission of Harper & Row, Publishers, Inc.

For an excerpt from *When I Have a Little Girl* by Charlotte Zolotow, Copyright © 1965 by Charlotte Zolotow. Reprinted by permission of Harper & Row, Publishers, Inc.

Designed by Barbara DuPree Knowles

Library of Congress Cataloging-in-Publication Data
Zolotow, Charlotte, 1915–
Everything glistens and everything sings.
Summary: An illustrated collection of poems arranged under eight subject categories including "The Sea," "People and Friendship," "Animals," and "Bedtime Thoughts."
1. Children's poetry, American. [1. American poetry]
I. Tomes, Margot, ill. II. Title.
PS3549.063E8 1987   811'.54   86–31917
ISBN 0-15-226488-4

Printed in the United States of America
FIRST EDITION   A B C D E

#15019063

CONTENTS

OBSERVING THE WORLD

I can't help seeing . . . I can't help dreaming

SCHOOL DAY

I don't mean to look
but I can't help seeing
a bit of sky outside the schoolhouse window.

I don't mean to watch
but I can't help watching
the maple branch that brushes against the pane.

I don't mean to dream
but I can't help dreaming
that I could be wandering
under the sky,
          watching the leaves
          watching the trees
          as the wind goes by.

THE TOP AND THE TIP

Hair is the top of a person,
a chimney's the top of a house,
a cover's the top of a book,
the tail is the tip of a mouse.

The sky is the top of the world,
the top of the sky is space,
a flower's the top of the stem,
the nose is the tip of the face.

IN THE MUSEUM

The horse from 200 B.C.
is made of stone,
but the way he holds his head
shows
someone long ago
loved a horse like him,
though now
both horse and sculptor
                    are dead.

THE TRAIN

I hear it
home in my bed—
somewhere out in the night
the cry of a train
flying through
the darkness.
      To where?
      To whom?

THE TRAIN MELODY

The train keeps on
with its chug chug song,
and on it is me
with my own melody:

    river   house   tree
    flower   fence   fisherman
    river   house   tree.

All these are in
my train melody.

Someone waves
and I wave back,
and the train chugs on
down the track,
chug chug chug
and on it is me
with my own melody:

    flower   fence   fisherman
    river   house   tree . . .

HALFWAY WHERE I'M GOING

Trains and boats and cars and wagons
are a way to go,
bikes and carriages and sleds
cutting through the snow.

Chairs and beds and sofas
are a way to stay,
swings and steps to sit on
for an ordinary day.

Sometimes I want to go away
to roam and roam and roam,
but halfway where I'm going
I always long for home.

THE BRIDGE

Glittering bridge,
curved like a harp
with your necklace of sparkling lights,
how you shine through the dark
of these silent summer nights!

THE FOG

Smoky with fog
the maples, the elms,
the dogwood along the driveway
stand cloudy and unseen.

From memory
I know they are there,
though there is nothing to see
but gray fog
covering the world
tonight.

THE SEA

the sound of the sea . . .
the waves and the spray

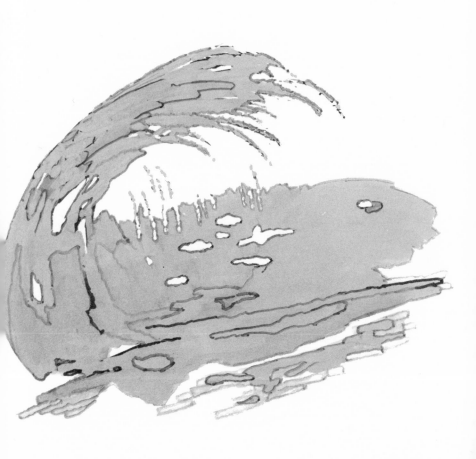

THE SEA

Muffled thunder
surging from the sea . . .
that gigantic white-laced wave
is tumbling straight to me!

BY THE SEA

The salty wind,
the sound of the sea,
the sand and the sun,
the waves and the spray—
a glistening, glittering
                    jewel of a day!

ABSENT FRIEND

A ship at sea
is a world at sea.
I hope it carries
you
     to me.

THE POND

I stood and watched
the smooth water
and saw myself
upside down.

The wind rose,
and suddenly
I became
a million zigzags
shimmering
in the sun.

In the morning it is green
with water lilies
like little moons
floating.

In the afternoon it is
broken into blue ripples
like ribbons.

At night
it is dark and mysterious
like a bowl
of black ink.

THE BOATS

Little white boats
moored on the lake,
what a wooden water sound you make.

The smooth blue water
looks so still,
but your wooden music plays
                    the wind's will.

THE RIVER

Quiver shiver,
golden river,
how you hold the sun!

Shimmer glimmer,
little waves,
showing day is done.

SUMMER SNOW

An evening by the sea
just before night
the fishing pier turned
a feathery white,
a lovely, soft white,
just as though
all those gulls
were summer snow.

COLORS

. . . a small rainbow in the sun!

BEETLE

Shining Japanese beetle
eating the rose,
how your wings
glisten
like a small rainbow
in the sun!

CANDLELIGHT AND MOTH WINGS

Candlelight and moth wings
gulls flying high
waves in the sea
clouds in the sky
snowdrops and snowstorms
phlox and birch trees
moonlight at night . . .
all these are white.

THE CARDINAL

After the snow stopped
the garden was white
and sparkled like crystals of sugar.
Whiteness was everywhere
except for one bird,
a cardinal,
like a drop of blood
in the snow

RED

Red is a good color.
                    Red
as strawberries
and cherries
and tomatoes.
              Red
as zinnias
and fire engines
and Christmas ribbons.
                      Red
as autumn leaves
and poinsettias
and hollyberries.
                  Red
as the heart of a rose.

Green is a good color.
     Green
as windowboxes full of ivy
and fern in the woods
and shutters on a white house.
      Green

as parrot feathers
and pine trees
and pistachio nuts.
    Green

as limes
and leaves
and little caterpillars.
     Green
as the grass itself.

YELLOW

Yellow is a good color.
                    Yellow
as canary birds
and calla lilies
and cats' eyes shining in the dark.
                              Yellow
as buttercups
and spires of goldenrod
and dandelions
and daisy hearts.
                    Yellow
as the sun itself.

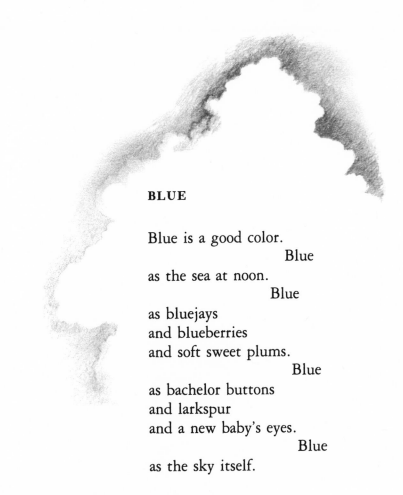

BLUE

Blue is a good color.
                    Blue
as the sea at noon.
                    Blue
as bluejays
and blueberries
and soft sweet plums.
                    Blue
as bachelor buttons
and larkspur
and a new baby's eyes.
                            Blue
as the sky itself.

GRAYNESS

Fog on the river
fog in the trees
gray mist moving
the golden leaves.

Willow bending,
dancelike,
long arms trailing
trancelike.
Gray morning
gray light
gray mist
gray night.

PEOPLE AND FRIENDSHIP

*Some people touch your hand
and music fills the sky.*

PEOPLE

Some people talk and talk
and never say a thing.
Some people look at you
and birds begin to sing.

Some people laugh and laugh
and yet you want to cry.
Some people touch your hand
and music fills the sky.

FALSE START

Just as I reached out my hand,
wanting you to play,
just as I knew I liked you
was when you walked away.

THE NEW GIRL

I can feel
we're much the same,
though I don't
know your name.

What friends
we're going to be
when I know you
and you know me!

SOMEONE I LIKE

Someone I like is far away,
I feel the silence everywhere.
I didn't know how much I'd care.
Someone I like is far away,
I feel the silence in the air,
I feel it, feel it
                everywhere.

LOOK

Firelight and shadows
dancing on the wall.
Look at my shadow
     TEN FEET TALL!

MY MOTHER

My mother is soft
with a pillow smell
powdery and warm.
She is like a fragrant tree
holding out her arms to me.

WHEN I HAVE A LITTLE GIRL

When I have a little girl
I will never say to her,
"When you are a mother
you will understand
why all the rules
are necessary."

"We'll see," my mother says
and smiles.

MY FATHER

My father is tall
and strong as a giant.
I bet
with his bare hands
he could break rocks in half.
But when I told him this one day,
he picked me up
and held me close
so that I *felt* his tenderness and
the rumble of his laugh.

A DATE

A little girl says,
"I love my mother,
but
someday
my father and I are going to the zoo
alone.
My mother will kiss us both good-bye,
BUT SHE'LL STAY HOME!"

TO THE ZOO

TOWARD DARK

There is a certain grind of brakes,
the slam of a car door,
the crunch of gravel underfoot
and
Daddy's home once more!

HALLOWEEN

The moon is full and
the night is strange,
filled with mystery.

From the shadows
under the tree
three small white ghosts
are coming up the walk
to me.

THE BRIDE

I wonder if ever
I will be a bride
with a white lace gown,
standing in front of everyone
looking beautiful
because someone
loves me
that much.

ANIMALS

Quivering and alive

BLACK DOG

Once when I was pondering
things I couldn't understand,
suddenly I felt
a wet nuzzling in my hand.

Oh, little furry dog,
the things I wish I knew
are probably simple
to loving souls like you.

LITTLE ORANGE CAT

Little orange cat,
you prowl
like a small tiger
(stalking what?)
in the field
of white daisies
and shining
buttercups.

RACCOON

Raccoon,
with your black ringed eyes
and tiny paws,
startled at your work,
to you my garbage can
is full
of treasure.

LYING IN THE GRASS

Lying in the grass
looking up through the trees
at the sky,
I saw a small bird
flying over the trees
high high high.

He dipped and he swooped
and flew to rest
on the branch of the tree
far above me.

And watching him
as I lay there,
    I wondered
if he could see
lying in the grass
looking at the sky,
something odd to him
which was
                me!

FIREFLY

On a June night
I once saw
a small dart of fire
burning in the honeysuckle bush,
flashing, flickering,
then flying slow and low
in the darkening world.

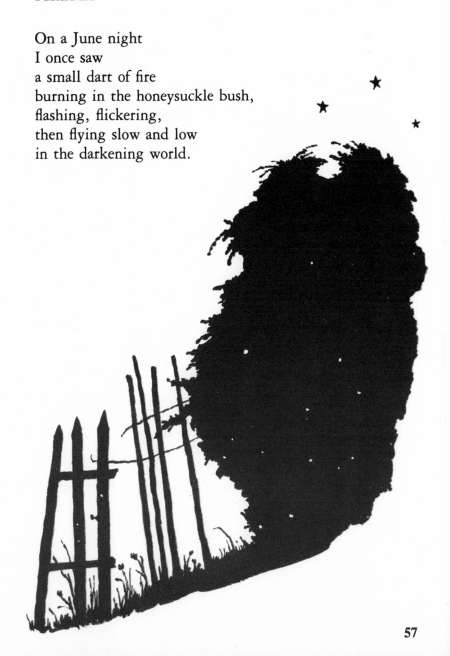

THE FLY

I was sitting on the porch
reading my book
in the summer sun.

A fly
settled on my page
black as ink.

Quivering and alive,
rubbing one leg against the other,
he sat on a word.

LADYBUG

Little ladybug,
with your
glazed red wings
and small black polka dots,
you look
like a
porcelain statue
until
suddenly
you
fly
    away.

LITTLE BIRD

Little hurt bird,
in my hand
your heart beats
like the pound of the sea
under the warmth
of your soft feathers.

LEOPARD IN THE ZOO

The lovely leopard
dreaming of
the dark jungle
       and tangled vines,
       monkeys and
       hot moist days,
doesn't care
about children
who stare
      wondering
         what
          he
           dreams

OUTSIDE AT NIGHT

In the autumn night
there is a huge harvest moon,
and two deer
stand side by side
at the dark stream
drinking the
moon's reflection.

THE SEASONS

It's hard to remember

THE SPRING WIND

The summer wind
is soft and sweet,
the winter wind is strong,
the autumn wind is mischievous
and sweeps the leaves along.

But the wind I love the best
comes gently after rain
smelling of spring and growing things,
brushing the world with feathery wings
while everything glistens and everything sings
in the spring wind
after the rain.

SPRING DAY

The sky is blue today.
The world looks new today,
new and very gay.

The trees are green today.
The world seems clean today,
clean and very gay.

The sun is bright today,
bright and very light today,
light and very gay.

It is a lilting day,
a fine and tilting day,
tilting and very gay today.

The world seems young and new.

THE DANCERS

The long yellow branches
of forsythia
and the white arms of spirea
move together
and then apart
in the light spring wind
like dancers
swaying, dipping,
to the sunlit music
of the air.

THE FIREFLIES

On summer nights
the fireflies
make starry earth
instead of skies.

The stars, I guess,
belong in the skies.
How nice on earth
there're fireflies!

AUTUMN

Now the summer is grown old,
the light long summer
                    is grown old.
Leaves change
and the garden is gold
with marigolds and zinnias
tangled and bold,
blazing blazing
orange and gold.
                The light long summer
                is grown old.

THE LEAVES

The world is weeping leaves today
golden, crimson, brown,
drifting slowly down.

Lovely autumn, please do stay
here in this little town!

The world is weeping leaves today,
golden, crimson, brown.

WINTER DAY

The world seems cold today.
Tomorrow it may snow.
In a strange and wary way
the world seems cold today,
white and very old today,
as though its pulse were low.
The world seems old today.
Tomorrow it may snow!

THE FIRST SNOW

There is a special kind of quiet
that each of us knows.
We hear it in our sleep
the first night it snows.

The silence stirs behind our dreams.
Something lovely calls.
Softly we wake to whiteness
as the first snow falls.

CONTRAST

As I watch the snow fall,
big, slow white flakes
like feathers floating down,
my hands are cold.

It's hard to remember
the summer
and soaking up the sun,
feeling its warmth
seep through me
deep through me
down to these frozen toes.

NOEL

Snow bright
crystal white,
magic light,
  the season of love is here!

The music of bells
sweet and clear
rises high
like flocks of birds
across the sky,
caroling caroling
sweet and clear.
  The season of love,
  the season of love is here!

NORTH AND SOUTH

Christmas again,
holly and pine,
bells and berries,
things that shine.

Christmas again,
but far away
palm trees drip
with ocean spray!
Far away it's very sunny
but here it's cold and white . . .

it's funny.

HERE

In this spot
covered now by snow,
tangled branch and twig,
in this spot where the ice edges
and the ground is frozen
and the birds peck at bread,
in this spot
there will be
crocuses blooming
yellow and white,
holding petaled cups
of sun,
if only
spring would
come.

GROWING THINGS

. . . all a garden needs

PANSIES

Pansies purple
pansies blue
their funny faces
remind me of you.

For whether they're yellow
or reddish or blue,
they seem to be smiling
just like you.

WEEDS

I can't understand
people who hate weeds.
Dandelions and buttercups
and clover for the bees
and maybe some Queen Anne's lace
are all a garden needs.

BUTTERCUPS

There's nothing so golden,
nothing so gay,
as fields of buttercups
on a sunny day.

CROCUS

Little crocus
like a cup
holding all that sunlight up!

THE HEDGE

The hedge,
a stiff brocaded lady,
stands fragrant
after the storm,
lacy with spiderwebs,
glistening with raindrop jewels.

TREES

The trees toss their long branches
making a shadow
of lace
in the sunlight,
whispering
the song
of forgotten winds.

THE APPLE TREE

Near that rusty
railway track,
an ugly junky scene,
blooms a little
flowering tree
radiant as a queen.

MARIGOLDS

I speak quietly of the marigolds
on the dark dining room table.
I do not sing
of their burst of brilliant orange and yellow
this early fall day
when outside the trees are changing to gold.
I speak quietly,
I do not sing,
I whisper, for beauty
is a fragile thing.

BEDTIME THOUGHTS

Good night, good night,
the golden sun is down

THE BED

When I am in bed,
I hear
footsteps of the night,
sharp,
like the crackling of a dead leaf
in the stillness.

Then my mother laughs
downstairs.

MOONLIGHT

The moon drips its light
honey-gold
into the darkness.

Silently
it quivers in the grass,
warmly
it lights the dew,
heavily
it rests
in the heart of the rose.

EIGHT O'CLOCK

There are times
when I hate to hear,
"It's eight o'clock,
bedtime, dear!"
Those are the nights
when the day has been long
with nothing to do
worth a song.
Those are the nights
when I hate my room
and when "eight o'clock" sounds
like the voice of doom.
But other nights
when I've played all day,
I almost wait
until I hear,
"It's eight o'clock,
bedtime, dear!"

GOOD NIGHT

We turn out the lights
and the color is gone.
The shapes are gone.
The desk,
the chair
with tomorrow's clothes laid out,
the books
in the bookcase,
the crayons
on the floor,
the bright curtains,
the red rug
are covered by friendly dark.

Only with closed eyes
can you see now.

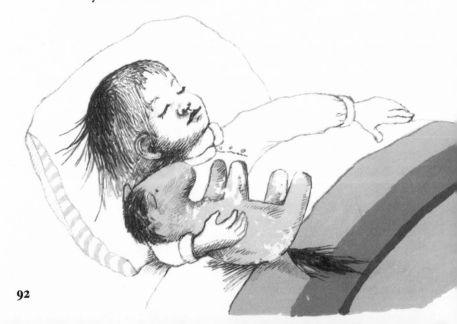

AGAIN GOOD NIGHT

Good night, good night,
the golden sun is down,
the purple sky deepens,
the moon is pale.

Bird song is silent,
the trees sigh,
and far away
a train rushes through the night.

Good night, good night.
The grownups talk quietly
downstairs.
The bedroom is cool and dark.

Good night, good night, good night.
Warm from your bath,
sleep toward the sweet dreams
the night will bring.

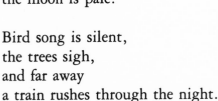

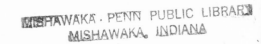

SLEEPLESS NIGHTS

One night
when I was very little,
I couldn't sleep.

My mother came
and carried me downstairs
and stood with me
looking out of our window.

The street light was on outside,
and snow was whirling, swirling,
a dazzling white
around and around the street light.
And the ground
and trees
and bushes
were icy crystal white.

I remember that night,
with the snow
white, white, white,
and my mother's arms around me
warm and tight.

INDEX OF TITLES AND FIRST LINES